The Trail Home

by Adam McClellan

illustrated by Lyle Miller

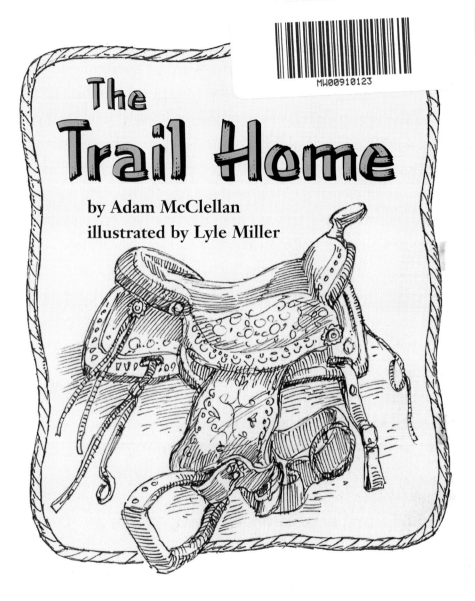

 HOUGHTON MIFFLIN BOSTON

It was a late June morning and I heard birds singing in the trees outside my bedroom window. From the window I could see the summit of the nearest mountain, still white with snow even now. Here in the Colorado Rockies, summers are cool and start late.

I was about to call to Mom and tell her I'd be right down for breakfast, but then I remembered that she had gone to visit Grandma in Idaho. I let Dad sleep in and went out to feed our animals. As I put hay out for the horses, I noticed the gate was ajar. Our Arabian horse, Hershey, was missing! I realized instantly that I had forgotten to latch the gate the day before. I knew Hershey enjoyed munching grass in a field high on the mountain, so I saddled my horse, Lindsay, and headed up there. I figured I'd get back home before Dad woke up.

When I started out, there were a few gray clouds hovering in the sky, but I ignored them. I followed the trail up to the field where I thought I'd find Hershey. I found bear tracks and a deer skull, but no sign of a horse. After checking a few more of Hershey's favorite spots, I turned around.

I was just heading home when the wind began to pick up.
To the west, the sky was darkening, and over the mountain
clouds were swirling. I nudged Lindsay, and she picked up her
pace.

Suddenly I thought I heard Dad's voice calling my name.
It must be my imagination, I said to myself. *Dad's probably still
asleep.* Then I heard my name again. I turned around and saw
Dad mounted on his horse, Cody. He was waving and calling
to me from an open ridge a short distance away.

"Dad!" I cried, but the driving wind threw my voice back at me. I grabbed the saddle horn firmly and stood in the stirrups, waving wildly to let him know that I had heard his calls.

Dad spurred Cody toward me. I dug my heels into Lindsay's sides, and she broke into a gallop. We quickly closed the wide gap between us. "Yvette, what are you doing up here? A storm's coming fast," Dad said, cocking his head toward the black clouds behind him. His serious expression made me nervous. "You know better than to go riding off when a storm's approaching."

I looked at the sky, now metallic gray above the dark blue mountains. "Hershey got loose, and I went looking for her. The storm kicked up while I was on the ridge."

Dad frowned and said, "Hershey will be spooked by this storm. She'll head for home as soon as it hits. We'd better get off this ridge before the sky lets loose!" As if on cue, drops of water started splattering against our jackets. The wind whipped the rain in all directions. We headed for a stand of trees, but the crazy swaying of the branches made the refuge unsafe.

Dad was telling me to keep moving when suddenly I heard a deafening crack. A heavy pine branch crashed down onto Dad, knocking him off his horse. Cody neighed fearfully, then bounded up the trail a couple hundred feet. There the horse stopped and looked back.

I jumped off Lindsay and ran to where Dad lay sprawled on the ground. His eyes were closed. "Wake up! Wake up, Dad!" I yelled, but he didn't respond. When I pulled at his collar, his eyes fluttered and opened. With my help, he struggled to a sitting position. I held my breath and waited to see what would happen when I let go. Dad seemed fine for a moment, but when he leaned on his left arm, he moaned and fell back again.

Somehow I had to get Dad down the long, steep mountain to our house—and then to a hospital. Farther down the trail, I could see Cody eyeing us warily as another clap of thunder echoed across the mountains.

Cody was a strong and sure-footed horse, but he was also skittish. I knew I couldn't control him. What if he spooked and started racing down the trail with Dad on his back?

I would have to rely on my own horse, so I turned to her and softly called her name. Cautiously, Lindsay stepped toward me.

As I stooped over Dad, he stirred and looked up at me. At first his eyes didn't focus on my face. "Dad?" I said softly. "Dad, can you hear me? Do you know who I am?"

"Yvette? Where's Mom?" he mumbled. "My head really hurts."

I fought to keep my voice calm. "She's at Grandma's house, Dad. She left yesterday afternoon and she's in Idaho by now." I knew that I needed to get Dad to a doctor, fast. "Give me your right arm so I can help you stand up." Dad reached toward me, and I pulled him up. He leaned on me and we took a step together. At first I stumbled under his weight, but when I saw that Lindsay was waiting nearby, I gritted my teeth and straightened up. I put Dad's good arm over my shoulder and reached my arm around his waist, slowly guiding him to Lindsay.

Dad seemed to know instinctively what to do. He wedged his foot into the stirrup and climbed weakly into the saddle. But once in the saddle, Dad slumped forward. He lay slung across Lindsay's neck, eyes closed, as if he had fallen asleep at home on the couch.

I felt a pang of fear run down my spine. Would Dad make it? Would the journey back to the house be too much for him? I pushed those thoughts out of my mind and concentrated on leading Lindsay toward the trail. As we approached Cody, I realized that I wasn't close enough to grab his reins. I took a chance and led Lindsay past Cody as if he wasn't there. Soon I heard a shuffle and another set of hooves behind us. I sighed with relief, knowing Cody was going to follow us home.

I calculated it would take almost an hour to get down the mountain. I was counting on Lindsay to get us home, and I knew that each step would be difficult. Luckily the trail at this spot on the mountain was wide enough for me to walk comfortably beside Lindsay. The rain was still coming down, and I heard thunder roll across the hills behind me. *Hold on, Dad,* I thought. Lindsay picked her way down the hill, careful to avoid puddles and stones. Even with Lindsay's gentle walk, Dad moaned every time she stepped down hard. I rested my hand on her neck and whispered encouraging words in her ear.

Twenty minutes from home, a familiar shortcut dropped steeply down to the right off the main trail. The shortcut was little more than a long slide down the hill, leveling out behind our barn. Water from the storm had turned the shortcut into a slippery, muddy mess.

On a good day, I could always make the steep descent— but should I risk it now? I glanced at Dad, who still seemed unconscious, and quickly made up my mind. I started down the shortcut, holding Lindsay's reins. Then I felt my arm pulled stiff behind me. Lindsay stood firm on the trail.

I tried to coax Lindsay down the shortcut, but she wouldn't budge. I was wet and tired, and I just wanted to get Dad home safely. I grabbed both of the reins, stood in front of Lindsay, and tried to pull her down the shortcut. My horse still wouldn't move. Just then I noticed the river of mud running down the hillside. If Lindsay had gone down the shortcut, she probably would have slipped and dropped Dad. "You're right, Lindsay," I said. "We shouldn't risk it." I went back to the main trail. Behind me, Dad groaned in the saddle. "We're almost home, Dad. You can make it," I said, moving forward more quickly.

Finally I spotted the smaller, safer trail branching off toward home. Suddenly there was an explosion of thunder. Cody whinnied, reared, then bolted past us. His terrified whinnies echoed in the air after he had disappeared from sight. Lindsay jerked at her reins but quickly calmed down and stayed with me.

The last half mile of the trail seemed to take forever. My clothes were soaked, and my toes and hands were numb. Water ran down my face and stung my eyes. My feet were coated in a thick layer of mud, and each time I lifted a foot, it felt like there was a ten-pound weight attached to it.

Just when I thought we were never going to be there, we rounded the last bend. The farm spread out in front of us, and I had never been so glad to see home. I looked up at the front of the house. I knew that I'd never be able to lift Dad up the porch steps and into the house, so I turned Lindsay toward the barn. Cody was already in front of the corral, snorting and stamping, impatient for us to join him. Rearing up next to Cody was Hershey! She must have galloped down the mountain when the storm began.

I led Lindsay into the barn and carefully helped Dad onto some soft straw bedding. As soon as I knew he would be comfortable, I rushed inside the house, praying the storm hadn't knocked out the phone lines. Elated to hear a dial tone, I called the hospital. I explained what had happened, and the woman who answered promised to send an ambulance right away. Then I ran back to check on Dad.

I sat next to Dad in the warm, dry barn and held his hand. I was thankful that we'd made it down the mountain all right, but worried that the ambulance wouldn't be able to find us. Dad's moaning was getting louder. In another moment he had opened his eyes and was looking at my face.

"Yvette? Are we in the barn?" Dad asked. "What happened?"

"Yes, we're in the barn. A heavy branch fell on you up on the mountain," I explained.

"A branch? But how did you get me home?"

"I had some help, from Lindsay," I said, smiling. "I got you to stand up and then you mounted Lindsay almost by yourself. We walked you down the mountain, and Lindsay made sure that we took the best route. She was really great, Dad. Cody was spooked at first, but he followed us home."

Dad looked at me, amazed. "And what about Hershey?"

I explained that Hershey was waiting for us when we got down the mountain. "I'm sorry, Dad," I said. "This was all my fault, 'cause I left the gate open. I really messed up."

Dad looked up at me and shook his head. "You didn't mess up," he said. "You were only doing what you thought was the right thing. And you got us home. You were courageous, Yvette, and I'm proud of you. But next time wake me up before you go chasing one of the horses." Dad squeezed my hand and smiled.

In the distance I heard an ambulance siren. "Dad, I'm going to go guide the paramedics to the barn," I said. Dad nodded and let go of my hand. As I headed back outside, I noticed that the rain had stopped. The gray clouds were beginning to break up, and the sun was shining on the top of the mountain. I waved to the ambulance driver, and he pulled right up to the barn.

"Boy am I glad to see you," I said, grinning. "My Dad's right in here." The paramedics opened the barn doors, and I heard them talking to Dad. Help had arrived, and everything was going to be just fine.